To Noriko and Kenichi

First published in the United States in 2006 by Chronicle Books LLC.

Copyright © 2003 by Komako Sakai.
English translation © 2006 by Chronicle Books LLC.
Originally published in Japan in 2003 by Hakusensha.
All rights reserved.

Typeset in Wendy and Today Sans.
English text design by Anne Ngan Nguyen.
Manufactured in China.

Library of Congress Cataloging-in-Publication Data
  Sakai, Komako, 1966-
    [Ronpåa-chan to fåusen. English]
    Emily's balloon / by Komako Sakai.
      p. cm.
    Summary: A little girl's new friend is round, lighter than air,
    and looks like the moon at night.
    ISBN-13: 978-0-8118-5219-7
    ISBN-10: 0-8118-5219-9
    [1. Balloons—Fiction. 2. Friendship—Fiction.] I. Title.
    PZ7.S143943Em 2006
    [E]—dc22
                2005011283

Distributed in Canada by Raincoast Books
9050 Shaughnessy Street, Vancouver, British Columbia V6P 6E5

10 9 8 7 6 5 4 3 2 1

Chronicle Books LLC
85 Second Street, San Francisco, California 94105

www.chroniclekids.com

emily's
balloon

emily's
balloon

by Komako Sakai

chronicle books · san francisco

One afternoon, Emily got a balloon.

Oops!

The balloon was tied to her finger.

And then it came home with her.

Let's take that off.

Whee!

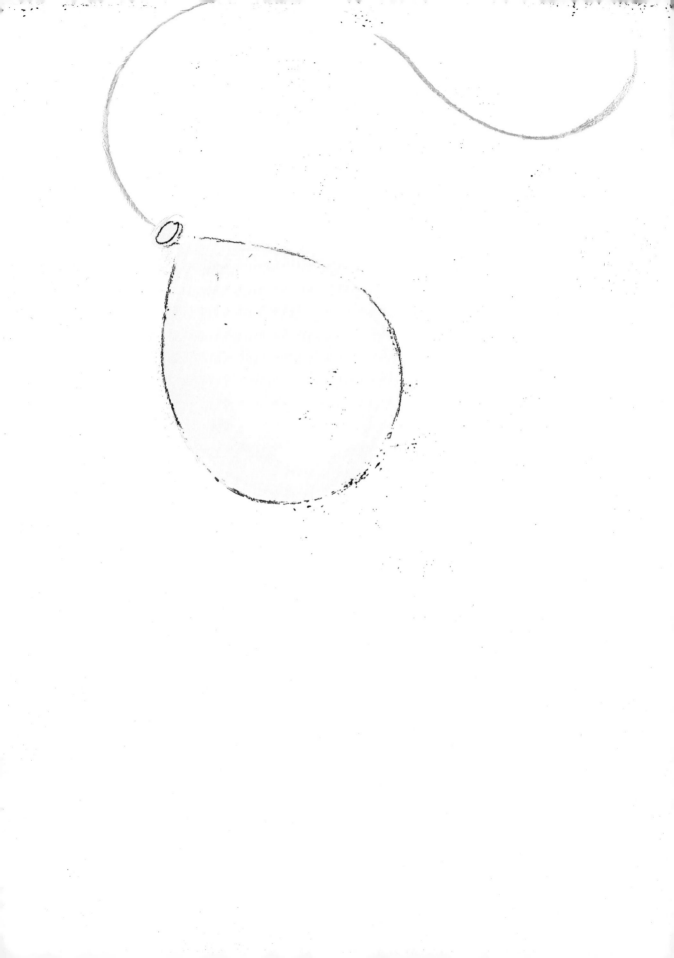

Uh-oh.

Here you go.

Again?

Emily's mother tied the string in a loop.

And put the loop around Emily's spoon.

Look!

It floats, but it doesn't fly away!

Emily and the balloon went into the yard.

They picked flowers.

Emily made a beautiful crown for the balloon,
and one for herself.

They played house.

Then *whoosh* went the wind.

The balloon! Emily's balloon!

There! In the tree!

It's stuck, Emily. I can't get it down.
I'm sorry.

Emily missed the balloon.
Dinner didn't taste good without it.

We wanted to eat together.

Then we would put on our pajamas,
and brush our teeth,

and go to sleep.

Tomorrow, I'll borrow a ladder and get it down.
  Really?
Really.
  Really and truly?
Really and truly. Goodnight, honey.

But Emily couldn't stop thinking about the balloon.
Was it still there?

She looked.
There it was, nestled in the tree.
It looked just like the moon.

Goodnight.